THE COOL BEAN

To Margaret Anastas & Kirsten Hall.
You two are the coolest of the cool.
—J.J. & P.O.

ISBN 978-1-338-75729-3

12 11 10 9 8 7 6 5 4 3 2 1 21 22 23 24 25 26

Printed in the U.S.A. 40

This edition first printing, January 2021

The artist used scanned watercolor textures and digital paint to create the illustrations for this book.

Typography by Jeanne L. Hogle

THE COOL BEAN

written by Jory John • illustrations by Pete Oswald

SCHOLASTIC INC.

BEANSIDE
ELEMENTARY SCHOOL
GO PODS GO!!!
HOME OF THE PODS

The *cooooool* beans.

Oh yeah . . . check out how they move.

Look at the way they swagger.

Notice their sunglasses. **YOW!**

The cool beans are known all over school.

From house to house.

Across town.

Beyond county lines.

In the olden days, last year,
we were all one big pod of beans.
We were a mixed bag, but
somehow it worked.

Yep. Those were the good old days...

and then we stopped seeing each other as much.

That's just how it is sometimes. You spend less time together, even though you're not totally sure why.

I watched as the beans I knew so well—the beans from my own pod—became the cool beans.

Oh, they were *soooooo coooooool.*

One of them could play the guitar. **COOL.**

One of them could draw the best superheroes. **COOOOOOL.**

One of them could jump higher than any bean I'd ever known. **COOOOOOOOOL.**

ME?

Well, I mostly stayed the same.

Sure, I made some *small* changes.

I wore sunglasses.

I slicked my hair back.
"Too slick."
GEL
SPRAY
"Ow."
I strutted around.
I swaggered.
"Oof!"

I was still picked last for everything.

My clothes never seemed to fit.

I snorted when I laughed.

I walked into stuff.

I was an *uncool* bean, for sure.

I started thinking of myself as just a common bean with no special skills. I couldn't compete, so I didn't even try.

I'd *never* be a cool bean.

It seemed like there were two types of beans in the world.

There were the cool beans...

and the beans like me.

The days all blended together.

I lived my life and things were just . . . *okay.*

I took tests and ate lunches and mostly kept to myself.

The cool beans continued being cool.

I mean, sure, I missed them. A bit.
But it's not like I was going to *say* anything.
I felt like all that coolness had gotten in the way of our friendship.

And that's how it went. . .
until one day.

I was in the cafeteria. I dropped my lunch on my loafers.

But then something sort of miraculous happened.

Out of nowhere, one of the cool beans helped me clean it up. He didn't even say anything. He just gave me a nod. That was it.

Later, I was out on the playground. I tripped and scraped my knee and maybe cried a little bit and everybody saw it.

Another one of the cool beans came to my side . . .

and, without a word, he dusted me off.

That afternoon, I was sitting in class. I wasn't really paying attention.

I didn't notice, but our teacher had called on me. Everybody stared. I sat there in silence. Nobody said anything.

And then . . .
then . . .
everybody just laughed!
At me.
That was it. After today,
I was officially a *has-bean.*

But then one of the cool beans stood up and came over to me. Everybody watched.

She leaned in close and whispered, "Hey. The teacher asked you to read from page 32." Then she gave me a quick wink and went back to her seat.

It was a small gesture, sure . . .

but it was also *everything.*

I walked home with a goofy smile on my face.

I smiled all the way through dinner.

That day made all the difference.
It was a day that could've been really bad, if not for the kindness of a few cool beans.

It gave me a shred of confidence. That shred of confidence has continued to grow.

Somebody had my back.

Or . . . a *few* somebodies.

After that, I started hanging out with the cool beans again.

Not all the time.
But sometimes.

At lunch.

After school.

Even on the weekends.

Throughout all of this, I realized that it's not about how you look or any of that other silly stuff.

It's about a wink or a nod or a smile at just the right moment.

It's about dusting somebody off, helping them up again, and pointing them in the right direction.

"You need a hand?"

"Yes, please."

Now *that's* cool.

JORY JOHN is a #1 *New York Times* bestselling author and two-time E. B. White Read Aloud Honor recipient. His books have won numerous state book awards and have been translated into more than twenty languages. Jory's work includes the *New York Times* bestselling picture books *The Bad Seed* and *The Good Egg*; the award-winning Goodnight Already! series; *That's What Dinosaurs Do*; the popular picture books *Penguin Problems* and *Giraffe Problems*; and many other books. He lives in Oregon.

PETE OSWALD is the #1 *New York Times* bestselling illustrator of *The Good Egg* and *The Bad Seed*, written by Jory John. The bestselling duo also created *That's What Dinosaurs Do* together. Pete is the cocreator of *Mingo the Flamingo* and works on numerous highly successful animated franchises as a character designer, concept artist, and production designer. He lives in Los Angeles with his wife and three sons.